I0621308

Zugzwang (a short story)

JJ Toner

Published by JJ Toner, 2025.

Zugzwang
A short story by
JJ Toner

First published April, 2015
Cover: Anya Kelleye
Smashwords edition
eBook ISBN: 9781908519221
Paperback ISBN: 9781908519924

Chapter 1

On March 3, 1933, four days after the burning of the Reichstag in Berlin, Kriminalkommissar Saxon of the Munich police arrived at work late. He'd had little sleep. His wife, Ruth, had spent half the night nursing a colicky baby in their one bedroomed apartment in Piperstrasse.

His telephone was ringing as he approached his desk. He picked it up and barked, "What is it?"

"You will be aware of this morning's murder in Schwabing." It was Saxon's boss, Kriminaldirektor Mydas.

"Of course, sir, a most unfortunate murder." Saxon signalled wildly to his assistant who had just entered the room balancing a couple of cups of coffee on a tray. Kriminaloberassistent Glasser put down the tray, grabbed the incident log from the front desk, and dropped it in front of Saxon. Saxon ran a finger down the overnight entries and found the incident in question.

Mydas grunted. "That's not how I would have described it. But I've decided it would be best if you take over the case. We need to find this maniac and put him away quickly. It won't take the newspapers long to make the connection between the two killings. And when that happens every woman in Munich will be too terrified to venture into the streets, and we will all come under extreme pressure from our political masters. Bernd Hessel has the two files. Drop into my office when you've read them."

Mydas terminated the call. Saxon groped for his coffee, his eyes glued to the incident log. "Why was I not told about this?"

Glasser used a bony finger to slide Saxon's coffee under his searching hand. "The report came in at 2:00 am, sir. The duty sergeant called Kommissar Hessel. I expect he thought you probably needed your sleep – you and your good lady, both."

One look at the preliminary notes from the crime scene told Saxon what connection the newspapers would make. A prostitute had been the subject of a gruesome murder in Hofgraben in the red light district a couple of weeks earlier. The mutilations sounded remarkably similar. "He should have called me. Do we have the victim's name?"

"Frau Henrietta Happeck, aged 59. She was a housekeeper for a Jewish banker."

More than any man Saxon had ever met, Glasser resembled the grim reaper. A tall man, he was nothing but skin and bone, all he needed was a hooded cape and a scythe. His voice had a hollow, echoing tone, too, the words 'Jewish banker' sounding like a death knell from his mouth.

#

Bernd Hessel was surprisingly cooperative.

"I've been asked to take over the red light case now that it looks like a double murder," said Saxon.

"I heard. Kriminaldirektor Mydas informed me this morning. I have assembled everything from both cases in these files."

Saxon took the files. The first one was unexpectedly bulky for such a recent case.

"I'm sorry for stepping on your toes, my friend..."

"Don't give it a second thought. And please let me know if there's anything I can do to help. Just be sure to catch this monster before he kills any more women." Hessel's pale, round face always appeared cherubic, his smile cold; today's angelic beam was warm and genuine, but strangely unsettling.

Saxon opened the first file. The photographs turned his stomach. Maria Kazinski, aged 24, had been disembowelled and decapitated 9 days earlier. She was naked. Whoever had done this had meant to obliterate her. Leaving her remains in a public place the killer had removed every vestige of humanity from the poor girl. It was a crime of pure evil, an act of undiluted hatred.

"She was Polish?" said Saxon.

"Originally, yes."

"A street walker?"

"No. She worked in a brothel. It's all there in the file."

Saxon turned a few pages and found the written record of the interview with Maria's roommate, Tania. Both girls worked in a registered brothel called Angel Wings located within 200 metres of the murder site.

He opened the second file. It contained very little more than the name and address of the victim: Frau Henrietta Happeck, housekeeper, Mozartstrasse 20. The photographs showed a remarkably similar crime. The age of the second victim made the pictures even more nauseating. It was like looking at the mutilated remains of your own mother.

#

Kriminaldirektor Mydas peered into his silver cigarette case and picked one out with the care of a man selecting a delicacy from a box of chocolates. "Take a seat, Kommissar. I take it you've read both files?"

Kommissar Saxon remained standing. "Why give these murders to me? You know I'm under pressure at home. Ruth has her hands full with a young baby."

Overweight and with a fondness for his beer, Mydas was not so much a policeman these days as a burnt out local government official, his chair moulded to the form of his fat behind, his eyes firmly fixed on his retirement. He flipped open his gold lighter, lit his cigarette and snapped the lighter shut. "What can I say, Saxon? The SS have been on the telephone already, demanding results. And you are my best investigator, after all."

"I was hoping for some leave..." Saxon crossed his arms.

"All leave is cancelled. For God's sake, sit down, man." He waved his cigarette like a smouldering dagger. "You know I have to give you this case. Who else do I have?"

"Bernd Hessel."

Mydas snorted smoke through his nostrils. "Kommissar Hessel is a fine policeman, but he's too slow. If you're asking me would I trust him with a case this important, the answer is no. No, it's your case now."

"Who do I report to, SS-Standardtenführer Kratschik or you?"

"You report to me, as usual. I will keep the SS informed."

#

The sandstone terraces in Mozartstrasse appeared like a monumental golden ingot in the evening sunlight.

Glasser laughed mirthlessly. "It seems not everyone suffered in the financial crash, boss." He switched off the engine. "People like that have brought this country to its knees..."

Saxon laid a heavy hand on Glasser's arm. "Wait in the car." He squeezed Glasser's arm.

"You're serious?"

"Wait here. I won't be long."

Isaac Goldfarb opened the door dressed in an elaborate green frogged smoking jacket. For a banker he seemed ill at ease, as if unused to having strangers in the house. He led Saxon into the front parlour and stood at an awkward distance, leaving his visitor standing.

Saxon removed his hat. "I'm sorry for your loss, Herr Goldfarb." He ran his eyes over the furniture. Carved fruit was much in evidence in light cherry, maple and walnut pieces. A Jewish menorah with nine fresh candles held pride of place over the mantel. Saxon parked his behind on a chaise longue.

Goldfarb took a chair, his hands resting in his lap. "Yes. Thank you, Kommissar. It was a terrible shock, the way... the way she..."

They remained an uncomfortable distance apart. Saxon felt he had to raise his voice to be heard. "How long was Frau Happeck in service with you?"

"A year and a half. She was an excellent housekeeper. I don't know how I'm going to replace her..."

"She lived here, in this house?" Saxon touched the side of his head; Goldfarb mirrored the movement. Saxon put the banker in his mid forties, tall, erect, with a full head of hair.

"Yes."

"Do you have other servants?"

"None. Frau Happeck is – or was – the only one."

"What was she doing out of the house at such an early hour?"

"She liked to buy fresh vegetables from the market in Haydnplatz. She visited the market two days each week."

"Which days?"

"Wednesdays and Saturdays."

"Did she have family?"

"Her husband died in the War. They had no children."

Saxon said, "I don't suppose you have any idea who might have killed her." Not exactly an open question, but he was suffering from lack of sleep.

"None. I assumed it must have been the madman who murdered that girl two weeks ago. Unless..." He stood up. "Can I get you anything, Kommissar? Tea? Coffee?"

"Unless what, Herr Goldfarb?"

"Unless maybe someone was sending me a message..."

It took a couple of moments for Saxon to wrap that suggestion in any sort of logic. The rise of the Brownshirts had cast a shadow over Germany, and since Hitler's accession to power certain groups were under the spotlight. The Jews were top of the Nazis' list of *undesirables*. "You're suggesting the killing might have been political?"

Goldfarb shrugged. "Henrietta came to me direct from Prinzregentenplatz 16."

The address rang a loud bell in Saxon's head, but he failed to make the connection. Rather than show his ignorance, he nodded. Goldfarb nodded back.

"Has anything else out of the ordinary happened recently?"

"Who can say these days? Everything seems out of the ordinary."

"What do you mean?"

Goldfarb's shoulders drooped. He looked older than his years. "Everything has changed. We've lost a lot of friends in the past year. This was our town. We used to throw parties." He gave a small laugh, shaking his head. "It's not safe for us in the streets. There are Brownshirt thugs everywhere, and they all seem to know who we are."

"You think the Brownshirts could have killed your housekeeper?"

Goldfarb ignored the question. "My wife... She's taken it very badly. I fear for her mental health."

Saxon gave the banker a moment to gather himself. Then he said, "I'd like to see Frau Happeck's room."

Goldfarb led Saxon to a room at the back of the house, opened the door and ushered him in.

"Thank you, Herr Goldfarb." Saxon waited by the open door, making it plain that he wished to be left alone.

Goldfarb left, and the Kommissar conducted a thorough search of the room. Henrietta Happeck was a tidy soul, with a neatly made bed, and everything in its proper place. The absence of photographs or letters spoke volumes. This woman was alone, isolated, probably lonely. Her housekeeping duties were her life.

Glasser had filled the car with cigarette smoke. "How was Herr Goldfarb?"

"Worried. Frightened."

Glasser suppressed a smile. "His sort always fall on their feet. But for his sake I hope he has his bags packed."

When Saxon mentioned Prinzregentenplatz 16, Glasser said, "That's where our Führer lives."

Of course! Frau Happeck used to be Hitler's housekeeper. Now that was a potential lead.

#

"Where to next?" Glasser edged the car into the traffic.

"The brothel. What was it called again?"

"Angel Wings." Glasser swung the car around, crossing the tram tracks and heading north.

They drove in silence for a few moments. Then Glasser said, "Why do you think you were given the case, Boss?"

"I'm sure the Kriminaldirektor had his reasons."

"You think it was his decision? The whole thing stinks to high heaven if you ask me."

"All right, spit it out before it chokes you." They were entering familiar territory. Glasser was a political animal, an early recruit to the Nazi Party, fully versed in the shenanigans of the Nazis.

"I'd say it was Standartenführer Kratschik's decision. This case is a classic poison chalice. Hessel has been earmarked for promotion. Nothing must be allowed to interfere with that. If you catch the killer, Kratschik will take the credit. If you fail you'll find yourself all alone watching your career disappear into the toilet."

Saxon grunted. He couldn't argue with Glasser's analysis, which was pinpoint accurate, as usual. As a member of the SS, Hessel was destined for greatness. His meteoric career spoke of favouritism and the eager greasing of palms. The undercurrent in Glasser's voice spoke volumes, too. He had been refused entry to the SS at least twice, probably because he lacked a gymnasium education.

They flashed their police badges at the door of the brothel and were shown into the Madam's private office.

An aura of cheap perfume announced Frau Bruckmann's arrival and accompanied her wherever she went. It was like an invisible shield, and every bit as effective. She nodded to Glasser, with whom she was obviously acquainted. Glasser introduced the Kommissar.

Saxon asked about Maria Kazinski. How long had she worked at the brothel? Did she have any special customers?

Frau Bruckmann inserted a black Russian cigarette into a ridiculously long cigarette holder. Glasser lit it for her; her arms weren't long enough to light it herself. "I've answered these questions already. Don't you policemen talk to one another?"

"Was she working on the night that she was killed?"

"Yes. She was here most nights."

"Who was she with that night?"

"That I can't tell you, Kommissar."

"Can't or won't?" said Glasser.

She turned on Glasser at that. "We don't keep records, and even if we did, our customers all use pseudonyms – as you well know."

"Did she have any difficult customers?" said Saxon.

"None, Herr Kommissar. All my customers pay in advance. And if you're asking me about violent customers..." she cut off Glasser's objection with an imperious wave of her cigarette holder, "...I really couldn't say. As long as my girls have no visible bruises, the clients can be as heavy-handed as they wish, and I never discuss the clients with the girls. Our customers are guaranteed absolute confidentiality." She turned her head, allowing her cigarette holder to point at Glasser for a second. "Idle talk is forbidden. The business wouldn't last a day if the girls gossiped about their clients."

Tania was a delight: tall and painfully thin, with long blonde hair tied in pigtails, and wearing a short skirt and tight blouse that left little to the imagination. Her only blemish was her fingernails which were chewed to the bone. Glasser invited her to sit. She did so, crossing her legs slowly. Saxon smiled at her and asked if she had any idea who could have killed her roommate.

Tania was tongue-tied. Eyes brimming with tears, she shook her head. Her chin trembled. The way her pigtails bounced on her bare shoulders with the movement of her head sent a primitive shimmer through Saxon's bones. He gave her a minute to regain a measure of composure.

"Do you know who she was with that night?" said Glasser.

She shook her head again, emphatically.

"Did she ever speak of any violent customers?" said Saxon.

"We never talked about the men."

"Never?" This seemed unlikely, in spite of what Frau Bruckmann had said.

"Look, we had better things to talk about than our work. We put all that behind us when we left here each morning. She was a good roommate – the best. I miss her so much."

Saxon said, "Who was her last customer that night?"

Her eyes opened wide in terror. Saxon was unsure if she had been touched by the horror of what her friend had endured or if there was something else troubling her.

"H... Heinrich. He calls himself Heinrich."

#

The next day was Saturday. Saxon spent the day with his wife and child. He tried pushing all thoughts of the investigation to the back of his mind, but the name 'Heinrich' rattled around like a marble in his skull.

In the early evening, Glasser parked outside the apartment and knocked on the door.

Saxon opened the door and said in a loud voice, "Yes, Glasser, I understand. Wait here while I get my coat."

Ruth glared at her husband. "You're not leaving me again? It's Saturday night! Surely you're entitled to some sort of home life."

"I'm sorry, dear. Something's come up. I have to go out for a few hours." He planted a kiss on her cheek and made a quick exit.

"You did warn Ruth that we were going on watch tonight?" said Glasser.

"Get in the car."

They stopped off at police headquarters where Glasser went in search of a camera.

"How are Ruth and the boy?" said Glasser when they were both back in the car.

'The boy.' Even Ruth called him 'the baby'. It was high time they settled on a name.

"They are well, thank you."

Glasser parked the car opposite the entrance to Angel Wings and they settled down to keep watch.

They had agreed with Frau Bruckmann that she would signal them if and when 'Heinrich' made an appearance.

Glasser said, "What age would you say she was?"

"Frau Bruckmann? Anywhere between late forties and mid fifties, I'd say."

"I think she's a lot older. I meant Tania, the one with the peroxide hair." Glasser leered at the Kommissar.

It was a busy night in Angel Wings.

They watched the entrance, waiting for a signal from Frau Bruckmann. Glasser took pictures. They discussed the Hitler connection. Glasser felt there was nothing in it, nothing more than a coincidence. Unless the Kommissar was suggesting some connection between the Führer and a common prostitute! Saxon was happy to let Glasser win that argument for the moment. Tucking the lead away in his head like a precious jewel to be savoured later, he closed his weary eyes for a moment.

Glasser woke him with a shout in the dead of night. "Wake up! Boss, wake up."

Saxon grasped at the fleeting memory of a dream, but it was gone, leaving nothing behind but an image of peroxide pigtails and a sensation of anxiety. His body was cold. He wiped his eyes and peered out through the misted windows. He saw no one.

"Did we get a signal from the Madam?"

"No, but you'll never guess who just arrived!"

"Tell me. And tell me you have his photograph."

"Only the highest ranking SS officer in the south of Germany, SS-Standartenführer Karl Kratschik." He grinned like a skull. "And yes, I have his picture."

Chapter 2

Saxon was surprised that Glasser knew Kratschik by sight. Saxon himself had never met him – Kratschik was based in the SS headquarters in Schellingstrasse, on the other side of the city – but he had a strong mental image of the man: tall, silver-haired, wearing the black SS uniform and carrying a riding crop. He'd spoken to him on the telephone. Karl Kratschik's voice was always smooth as a baby's bottom. He spoke a brand of perfect German that came only from a privileged background and an expensive education in a private gymnasium. Saxon fancied he might sport a duelling scar on his left cheek.

Saxon wiped his eyes, stretched his limbs and offered to buy some food.

"Nothing for me, thank you," said Glasser.

Saxon bought Brötchen and Bratwurst for two from a street cart. "You've got to eat," he said to Glasser.

Glasser accepted the food. Saxon devoured his own, and watched his assistant pick at the bread. He never touched the sausage. The man was clearly an automaton. He needed no food – and no sleep.

#

As dawn broke, a suffocating fog descended on the city, making further photography impossible. Glasser drove Saxon home.

Saxon opened the front door of his apartment quietly. Ruth was in bed, the baby in the crook of her arm. Both were sleeping like angels. He leant down and kissed the infant's forehead. The child woke with a start, arms flailing, took one look at his father, opened his mouth, filled his lungs with air and screamed. And then all three were awake, Ruth chastising her husband for his stupidity while offering a breast to the infant.

13

With the baby guzzling milk, peace returned to the Saxon household. The boy was a picture of health. Saxon imagined he'd put on weight in the past 24 hours. Ruth, on the other hand, looked exhausted, eyes red-rimmed and bloodshot.

"Tell me why you couldn't have come home last night. What was so important that you had to leave me to cope on my own?"

"You've heard about the woman murdered in Schwabing? I've been given the case."

"Couldn't they give it to somebody else?"

"It's a high profile case, Ruth. I could be famous if I solve it."

"And what if you can't solve it? Not every case gets solved."

He made her breakfast, feeling guilty because he was neither hungry nor tired as he'd eaten and slept in the car. For Ruth's sake he would eat something and feign sleep.

Ruth put the sleeping infant back in his cot. Keeping her voice low, she said, "That man scares me."

"Who? Glasser? Because he's a Nazi?"

"Because he's so thin!"

Saxon nodded. "He eats like a bird. Sometimes I wonder what keeps him upright."

He dressed for bed and lay down beside Ruth. She rolled toward him, wrapping an arm across his chest. "I really needed you last night."

"I know. I'm sorry I left you alone with the baby."

She snuggled closer. He wrapped an arm around her and closed his eyes. Within minutes, Ruth was snoring on his chest. He remained wide awake.

#

The telephone rang early on Monday morning. Saxon leapt out of bed to answer it, afraid that it would wake the baby.

It was Glasser. "Good morning, Kommissar. I'm sending a car around to collect you. There's been another killing."

A small crowd had gathered at the junction of Moralstrasse and Glötzleweg, held back by two uniformed policemen.

"This one's a teacher," said Glasser. "Her name's Maxine Limburg."

"The method?"

"The same."

The body lay under a mature fir tree in Glötzleweg, covered in a sheet. At a signal from Saxon, Professor Valachek, the Medical Examiner, pulled the sheet back to reveal the headless corpse of a young woman, naked, the stomach ripped open. Saxon's Sunday night meal made a dash for freedom. He clamped his teeth shut and covered his mouth with a hand.

"The head's over there." Valachek nodded to his left where a blood-stained towel covered something. He took a step toward it. "Do you want to see it?"

Saxon swallowed his food for a second time. "No thank you. How do we know who she is?"

Glasser answered. "She was discovered by her husband, Erik. They lived just around the corner."

Saxon tried to imagine the shock of discovering Ruth like this. He shivered.

Professor Valachek gave an approximate time of death – no more than 2 hours earlier, between 5 and 6 am. "I may be able to tie it down more precisely when I get the body to the morgue."

Saxon and Glasser found the Limburgs' house in Hofbrunnstrasse. Erik Limburg sat in the kitchen surrounded by concerned friends and neighbours. They'd made him tea.

"I'm terribly sorry, Herr Limburg," said Saxon. "Do you feel up to answering a few questions?"

Limburg's hands shook so much he couldn't pick up his teacup without help. He nodded to Saxon.

"Do you have any idea who might have done this?"

Limburg shook his head.

"How long were you married?" asked Glasser.

One of the neighbours answered. "Six months."

Barely past their honeymoon, thought Saxon. "When did you last see your wife?"

Limburg found his voice. "Early this morning. There was a telephone call... She went out..."

"Do you know who the call was from?"

"She didn't say."

"What did she say?"

"She said she had to leave early – before breakfast. She usually makes – made – breakfast before she left for work..."

"What time was this?"

"Five thirty."

"Your wife was a teacher, I believe. Where did she work?"

One of the neighbours answered again. "Altenadler School for Boys."

They found Altenadler School for Boys on Lochhamer Strasse, a brooding redbrick building, its entrance hall dominated by a massive portrait of Martin Luther hanging on a wall. They showed their police badges to the caretaker who led them to the headmaster's office.

Glasser did the introductions.

Bart Freudl, the headmaster, a short man with a strong head of hair, dressed in coarse Bavarian tweed, looked at his watch pointedly. "I don't have much time to spare. The morning is the busiest time of the day for me. What's this about, anyway? I hope my seniors haven't been causing mischief again."

"It's nothing like that, sir," said Glasser. He glanced at Saxon.

Saxon said, "I'm afraid we have bad news, Herr Freudl. One of your teachers, Frau Limburg, has been found dead."

The headmaster's hand shot to his mouth. "Maxine? Oh, no! What happened? Was it a car accident?"

"Frau Limburg has been murdered," said Saxon.

The headmaster blanched. "That can't be. She was perfectly well yesterday."

"As I said, sir, she was murdered – early this morning."

"You mean someone killed her?"

"I'm afraid so, yes."

"But who would want to kill her? Maxine was well liked by everyone in the school – boys and teachers. I can't believe anyone would want to kill her."

True to type, the headmaster's first instinct was to question everything he was told.

Glasser said, "When did you see her last?"

"Yesterday evening, when she left the school at closing time."

"How did she seem?" asked Saxon. "Was she upset, anxious, in a hurry, anything like that?"

"No, she was her normal happy self."

"Did you call her on the telephone this morning for any reason?"

"No, although she is overdue. I would have called her number in the next half-hour if... if she hadn't... if you hadn't..."

"How long has she worked here in the school?"

"Eighteen months. Since October, 1931."

"Since before she was married."

"Yes. She was Maxine Weiss then."

"Where did she come from?"

"I'm not sure. She had a private teaching position somewhere."

"You never asked where?" said Glasser, a little harshly.

"I had no reason to."

Saxon asked for a photograph of Frau Limburg. Herr Freudl rummaged in his desk and found a picture of the senior class from 1932, taken in bright sunshine. He pointed out the smiling figure of Frau Limburg standing by his side to the left of the class. It seemed impossible that the bloody headless ruin Saxon had seen in Glötzleweg could be all that remained of this smiling woman.

"Thank you. I'll hold onto this," he said.

#

Back at the office, Saxon found a stranger dressed in an expensive Italian suit waiting for him. His first thought was that this was a banking friend of Goldfarb's, but when he saw the stranger's full length leather coat draped across the back of a chair, he stiffened. What business could the Schutzstaffel have with him?

"Kriminalkommissar Saxon?"

Saxon recognized the honey voice immediately. The SS man was older and shorter than Saxon expected. His broad face and distinctive square chin looked nothing like Saxon's mental picture, and there was no sign of a riding crop or a duelling scar on either cheek. "Herr Kratschik, good to meet you in person at last." He offered a smile and a hand.

Kratschik ignored the hand. "I was disappointed to hear that your killer has struck again so soon. And unfortunately the newspapers have connected the three deaths." He dropped a rolled up newspaper on Saxon's desk. It sprang open and Saxon read the headline:

KILLER STALKS THE STREETS OF MUNICH
3 WOMEN BRUTALLY MURDERED

"I have decided to take personal charge of the investigation. Now that the story has broken, it is all the more imperative that we find the killer before he strikes again."

"Kriminaldirektor Mydas—"

"— has been informed of my decision. For the remainder of the investigation, until the case has been resolved, you will report to me. Is that clear?"

"Perfectly, Herr Standartenführer."

Kratschik sat down. "You will start by briefing me on your progress so far."

Saxon sat at his desk, aware of an annoying tremor in his hands, its cause mostly anger, but there was a spoonful of fear mixed in there as well.

"We have spoken to the owner of the brothel where Maria Kazinski worked and also with her roommate, Tania. We have also interviewed Frau Happeck's employer, the banker Goldfarb."

"What of this latest victim?"

"She was a young schoolteacher, I have spoken with her husband and her headmaster."

"How many suspects do we have?"

"We have no obvious suspects, yet, sir, and nothing that might be called a positive lead."

"Have you spoken to the Medical Examiner?"

"I met him at the crime scene this morning."

"Did you discuss the three cases?"

"No, sir. There wasn't time."

"I'm disappointed, Saxon. Should you not be there right now? I would have thought the Medical Examiner's office would be at the very top of your list."

"Yes, sir."

"I want your very best work on this case, Saxon, do you hear me? And if you need more resources, please ask."

"Thank you, sir, but I have as much as I need for the moment."

#

Kratschik left, and Glasser took his place.

"What did he want?" said Glasser.

"We are now reporting to him until the case is solved. We must work harder."

"How does Herr Mydas feel about that?"

"The Kriminaldirektor has been informed. Is there anything in last night's photographs?"

"Nothing obvious, but I have a good clear picture of Standartenführer Kratschik."

"Keep that safe. It might be useful," said Saxon. "Give me the school photograph that Freudl gave us."

Glasser handed the picture over, and Saxon examined it under a magnifying glass. He pointed to one of the boys in the middle row. "Who does this remind you of?"

Glasser took the picture. "Kratschik! That chin is unmistakable. I'd bet a week's wages that this is Kratschik junior."

"Check it with the headmaster. I have to visit the Medical Examiner's office."

Glasser stopped at the office door. "You do realize if the boy in the picture is Kratschik's son, that will give us links between Kratschik and two of the three victims."

#

Professor Valachek had both hands inside Frau Limburg's headless cadaver. The blood smears reached his elbows. Kommissar Saxon asked him if he could shed any light on the case.

"What did you have in mind?" said Valachek.

"Anything that would help us to identify the killer. His motive, perhaps."

"Sorry, Saxon. I can tell you what killed each of the three women, but I'm a medical man. I have no skills in reading entrails. Hire a spiritualist or buy yourself a Ouija board."

Saxon asked to see the other two victims, and Professor Valachek peeled back two sheets without ceremony, revealing two decapitated corpses on adjacent tables. Saxon looked them over. He was not unfamiliar with the sight of death, but each of these bloodless cadavers had been the subject of a frenzied attack, and the separation of the heads was not easy to look at. He thanked the professor, and asked, "What of the sequence of events?"

"Frau Happeck was killed by a single blow to the back of the head. The mutilations were all post mortem. Fräulein Kazinski, on the other hand, was alive until the end."

"You mean the decapitation killed her?"

"Most likely, yes. The initial blow to her head would have rendered her unconscious, but it didn't kill her."

"What about our latest victim, Frau Limburg?"

"She was lucky. The mutilations were all inflicted post mortem."

The professor gave Saxon a copy of the first autopsy report and promised to send on the second and third as soon as they were complete. As he was leaving, Professor Valachek said, "I hope there won't be too many more like this."

The professor's tone suggested that he held Saxon to blame personally for the three killings.

#

A thin vestige of the early morning fog lingered in Munich's low-lying streets as Saxon drove toward the office the next morning, deep in thought. If Freudl confirmed that Kratschik's son was a student at the school last year, then that would link Kratschik to two of the victims, making him a suspect, not that he could report the fact to his new supervisor! Any link between Kratschik and Frau Happeck, no matter how tenuous, would almost certainly close the case.

Kriminaloberassistent Glasser had shown himself to be a customer of the Angel Wings brothel. If there was anything connecting him to either of the other two victims he too would have to be placed on the list of suspects and removed from the investigation.

The murder of Frau Happeck was the most puzzling. The other two victims were young women while Frau Happeck was beyond middle age. If the killer was a crazed sex maniac, as seemed likely, then the murder of Frau Happeck made little sense. That killing was surely the key to the whole case.

He turned the car around and headed back toward Prinzregentenplatz.

#

Saxon parked across the road from Prinzregentenplatz 16 and watched the comings and goings for a while. Two food vans and one from a flower shop made deliveries, and one Reichswehr dispatch motorcyclist delivered a parcel to the apartment building, but he thought that Adolf Hitler was not in residence. His personal SS guards were nowhere to be seen. Surely, the Führer was in the opera house in Berlin, where the Reichstag would be in session.

Hitler's armour-plated Mercedes Benz drove up and parked outside the apartment building. The driver got out and went inside. When he re-emerged carrying a bucket of water, Saxon got out of his car and walked across to talk to him.

He showed his police badge to the driver. "You are the Führer's driver?"

"His chauffeur. What of it?" He ran a finger across his moustache, indistinguishable from his master's. This was not a gesture of a nervous man, rather a signal of supreme assurance, as if the square on his upper lip possessed the spirit of the Führer himself.

Saxon snapped his fingers. "Your papers."

The driver handed over his identity card. It bore the name Julius Schreck.

Saxon said, "I am engaged in an active murder investigation. One of the victims, a Frau Happeck used to work here, I believe."

"I can't help you," said Schreck. He dropped a sponge into the bucket, splashing Saxon's trousers.

"Can you confirm that Frau Happeck worked as a housekeeper to the Führer until about 18 months ago?"

"I haven't been driving for the Führer that long. You need to speak with his previous driver, Emil Maurice."

"Where can I find Herr Maurice?"

The driver shrugged. He turned his back to Saxon and began applying soapy water to the car.

#

A quick check of the archives at headquarters produced police files for both Emil Maurice and Julius Schreck. A former watchmaker, Maurice had a long criminal record dating back to the Munich Beer Hall Putsch of 1923, when Maurice, Schreck and Adolf Hitler, were all jailed in Landsberg Prison. Maurice's SS number was 2.

Schreck was SS number 5. He had been a close friend of Hitler's since the foundation of the Nazi Party, and commanded his personal bodyguard for two years from 1925 to 1926.

Maurice's present whereabouts were unknown. Saxon put Glasser to the task of finding him, saying, "I'm going back to the brothel to speak with Tania again."

At Angel Wings, Tania quickly confirmed that Glasser was an occasional visitor to the brothel. There was nothing kinky about his sexual preferences and nothing unusually violent about his behaviour. Saxon showed her the school picture and asked her if any of the boys were patrons of the business. She pointed out several of the boys.

"This is Heinrich," she said, pointing to Kratschik junior.

"Is he ever violent?"

"It's more than my life's worth to answer that question." Tania flushed, casting her gaze down to her shoes.

"In confidence, Tania. I swear no one will ever know that you told me."

It took a few more minutes to persuade her to give him the information, but finally, she said, "The boy is a tiger. He has sharp claws and can be heavy-handed at times."

"How heavy-handed?"

"Very, and that's all I'm going to say on that subject."

As Saxon adjusted his hat to leave, Tania picked up the school photograph and pointed to it again.

"This man is a regular customer," she said.

Chapter 3

Glasser was open-mouthed. "Freudl, the headmaster of Altenadler School for Boys? I don't believe it."

"Tania picked him out of the school picture. That makes him a live suspect, since we can link him to two of the victims."

"But not the third."

Saxon listed his suspects on his fingers. "Kratschik senior, Kratschik junior, alias Heinrich the heavy-handed, and Freudl. We can link them all to the two young women."

"But none of them links to Frau Happeck," said Glasser, thoughtfully. "What about your fourth suspect?"

"What fourth suspect?"

"That miserable reprobate Glasser. You know he's a regular visitor to the brothel."

Saxon laughed at Glasser's solemn, straight-faced delivery. "If we included all the clients of Angel Wings, half the male population of Munich would be suspects."

"I assume you asked Tania about me."

"I did. She confirmed that you are always well behaved. You're not a suspect, not until I can link you to at least one of the other two victims."

Glasser gave his toothy grin. "I located Emil Maurice, Hitler's ex-driver. He's living in Innsbruck. Hitler fired him and he moved there immediately after Geli Raubal's suicide."

Saxon recalled the case of Geli Raubal. Hitler's niece and lover had committed suicide in Hitler's apartment in September, 1931. At the time, there were rumours, spread by his political opponents, that Hitler had murdered the girl, but murder was ruled out.

#

SS-Standartenführer Kratschik dropped in after lunch. Saxon told him that Freudl was now a suspect. He made no mention of his other two suspects.

Kratschik gripped his hands together as if in prayer. "Progress at last! But Herr Freudl? I know him, Kommissar. He's a most unlikely killer, headmaster of my son's old school, a pillar of the community."

"A pillar of the community who attends a brothel?"

"Good point, good point, and you must follow up on every possible suspect, leave no stone unturned until the madman has been apprehended. I'll arrange a search warrant for his home for this afternoon."

#

While they waited for the search warrant, Glasser fetched the Geli Raubal case file from the archives and gave it to Saxon to read.

The file consisted of a couple of pictures of the dead girl, and half-a-dozen sheets of paper: The Medical Examiner's report concluded that Geli had died at Prinzregentenplatz 16 on Friday, September 18, 1931 as a result of a single gunshot wound to the chest. The Examining Magistrate's determination was that the young woman had used Hitler's gun to take her own life. A statement from Hitler's chauffeur, Emil Maurice, was the basis for Hitler's alibi: he had driven Hitler to Nuremburg that day. They spent the night in a small hotel and had picked up a speeding ticket as they dashed back to Munich the following morning on receiving news of the tragedy. The file contained a copy of the speeding ticket. The housekeeper, Frau Happeck, had given a statement as she had discovered the body. Apparently no one had heard the shot.

A quick mental calculation told Saxon that Hitler's alibi was as watertight as a sieve with a large hole in it. He could easily have shot Geli Raubal on Friday and sped away north to spent the night at the Nuremburg hotel. Nuremburg was only two hours away.

Frau Happeck had left Prinzregentenplatz and joined the Goldfarb's household a month after Geli's 'suicide', in October, 1931.

#

Armed with a search warrant, and accompanied by four uniformed Orpo municipal policemen in a meat wagon, they arrived at Herr Freudl's home at dusk. Located in Feldafingerplatz, within easy walking distance to the north of the school, the 3-storey house had the look of something from the film *Nosferatu* with leaded windows, overhanging gables and encircling giant fir trees.

An elderly woman met them at the door and tried to bar their way. Glasser waved the warrant at her and pushed past into the hallway, followed by the uniforms.

Saxon asked the old lady to announce their arrival to the headmaster. She shuffled off to do his bidding while Glasser organised the search party.

When Freudl arrived he steered Saxon into a cavernous study, three of the walls lined with bookcases, floor to ceiling. They sat face to face by a cold fireplace.

Saxon presented the warrant. Freudl put on his glasses and read it slowly.

"And the reason for the search? You suspect me of some crime?"

"Tell me, Herr Freudl," Saxon replied. "Are you acquainted with a Frau Henrietta Happeck, a woman of middle years, a housekeeper?"

Freudl shook his head. "No, but I've seen the name in the newspaper. Wasn't she of one of the three murder victims?"

"Did you know her? Had you ever met her?"

"Never."

A stray thought scampered across Saxon's mind. Freudl had the look of a petty thief – the classic slack jawed stare and hollow smile of a life of crime. His eyes were too close together. His receding hairline suggested receding morals. The man could not be trusted.

"Who does your housekeeping?"

"Mother looks after the house."

"That was your mother who opened the door? It's a big house for one woman on her own."

Freudl laughed, "She may be old, but she's fiercely proud. She would never allow another woman into this house."

Saxon felt a twinge of pity for the man. "You're not married, Herr Freudl?"

"I've never had a wife."

"You have been seen at a brothel in Hofgraben."

Freudl coloured quickly. "I have to... I need... I'm sure you understand. But Angel Wings is fully registered. I have broken no law."

"Even so..."

"Even so, I know the school board would frown on the practice."

"Your feet wouldn't touch the ground," said Saxon with a blank face.

"They don't have to know, do they? I have broken no laws, after all." Freudl's eyes were pleading.

"They won't hear it from me," said Saxon, thinking he couldn't guarantee Glasser's silence. "Now tell me where you were on Thursday night."

"I was here, marking papers."

"Can anyone confirm that?"

"My mother. What are you accusing me of, Kommissar?"

"I am accusing you of nothing, Herr Freudl, but we must eliminate your name from our enquiries. Where were you on the night of Saturday the eighteenth of February?"

Freudl hesitated before answering. "That Saturday night I spent some time at... that place."

"Angel Wings?"

"Yes, but I wasn't there for more than a couple of hours. I was home and tucked up in bed by eleven."

"Your mother will confirm that?"

"Yes."

"Who were you with in the brothel? Were you with Maria Kazinski?"

"I don't recall, but it wasn't her."

"You're certain?"

"Positive. I was definitely not with Maria that night."

"But you've spent time with Maria on other nights?"

"Not often, but yes."

"And where were you last night?"

"I was here all night."

"Your mother will confirm that?"

"Yes, of course."

#

Saxon and Glasser sat at a quiet table in a tavern some distance from headquarters. The search of Freudl's house had revealed nothing but an unusual collection of exotic magazines hidden in a box in an attic.

Saxon paid for two steins of beer. "I won't be in the office tomorrow. I want you to keep things ticking over while I'm away."

"Where will you be, Boss?" said Glasser.

"I'm travelling to Austria tonight. I hope to talk to Emil Maurice in Innsbruck in the morning. I don't want the Standartenführer to know where I'm going, so I'll be relying on you to cover for me."

"Right, Boss."

The train journey from Munich to Innsbruck took four hours. Saxon was weary, and if it hadn't been for the spectacular scenery – the Austrian Alps, the precipitous viaducts spanning fast-flowing rivers – the clack-clack of the wagon wheels on the rails would have lulled him to sleep.

He had left an angry wife at home with a baby on one hip, a book of baby names on the other. She would finally have to choose a name by the weekend when they had an appointment with the pastor at his christening font. Ruth had had been hoping for a girl. She was caught unprepared when her baby arrived with that unexpected extra appendage.

Saxon turned his mind to the case. Of his three suspects, the SS man seemed the most likely, especially given the way that he had inserted himself into the investigation, presumably intending to interfere with the outcome. Of course, he might have done the same in order to protect his son. Freudl seemed the least likely candidate. There was no evidence against him and while living a life of enforced celibacy in a cavernous old house with an infirm mother was probably not good for his nerves, and dipping his quill in a house of ill repute was doing little to advance his career, nothing had suggested that he was a frenzied killer of women.

Surrounded on all sides by towering snow-capped mountains, Innsbruck was shrouded in perpetual mist. Saxon took to the streets on foot. Emil Maurice's address was not far from the railway station.

The city had an altogether Austrian feel, with brightly painted houses sandwiched together in narrow thoroughfares that owed much to the German style of urban planning. Hitler's grim portrait adorned every shop window. The women wore colourful flared dirndl skirts and aprons; some even wore lederhosen. And while Bavaria was no stranger to felt alpine hats, here every man seemed to wear one. Saxon felt conspicuous in his plain suit, police boots and Homburg.

Maurice was not at home. His landlady hadn't seen him for several days. Saxon explained that he was a distant cousin of Emil's on a walking tour. He had hoped to meet Emil before he continuing his journey. She suggested that Maurice might be found in Elferhaus, a popular beer cellar.

The beer cellar was full of happy drinkers. Saxon asked a young serving wench with a prominent mole on her upper lip where he might find his distant cousin.

"He's not in tonight, but it's early," she said. "What can I get you?"

He ordered a half-stein of the local brew.

As the night wore on the place filled to capacity. Saxon kept his half-stein topped up. He checked with his serving wench from time to time, but Maurice never appeared. At 11 pm, with drooping eyes, he picked two cards from the bar advertising a local hotel and handed one to her. They'd spoken so many times during the evening that Saxon thought of her as an old friend.

"I can't wait any longer. If you see Maurice, ask him to contact me here."

Returning to Maurice's lodgings, he gave the landlady the second card and the same message.

In order to avoid awkward questions about his lack of luggage, Saxon paid the hotel owner in advance for a room for a single night. He hadn't eaten for hours, but he was too tired to care. He called his wife on the telephone and listened to the account of her day. After the call he barely had enough energy to take off his clothes and climb into bed.

A knock at the door woke him in total darkness. He switched on a light and checked his watch: 4 am.

He went to the door and called out, "Who's there?"

When no one answered, he opened the door cautiously. The corridor was deserted, but someone had pushed an envelope under the door. Inside the envelope he found a single sheet of paper bearing the words: Valluga midday. It was signed with the initials E.M.

#

Maurice couldn't have chosen a safer place for a meeting. Valluga: the highest peak overlooking Innsbruck, reachable only by cable car. The gondola could carry no more than a handful of people at a time, and anyone in there would be clearly visible long before they arrived.

The journey to the peak took 2 hours in a succession of funiculars, each gondola smaller than the last, all swinging in the breeze at mind-numbing distances from the ground.

Saxon was accompanied to the top by three excited skiers, finally stepping from the gondola at the mountaintop in bright sunlight, gasping in the thin, icy air. The skiers dispersed, leaving the detective alone with the 360 degree panorama of the Alps and Innsbruck laid out below like a model village.

He climbed the last few metres to the rest station and stumbled inside, took a table by a window and ordered coffee. The clock on the wall read 12:10. Casting his gaze around, he checked out the 10 people sitting at the tables. Maurice was not among them.

At 12:45 he ordered a second cup of coffee. As the waiter moved away, a man approached wearing a ski suit and heavy boots. He sat at Saxon's table and removed his gloves. Saxon recognised Emil Maurice, older, more wrinkled and more tanned than the photograph on his Munich police file, but definitely him.

"My name is Saxon. Thank you for meeting me, Herr Maurice."

"Police?"

"Yes. I'm investigating the recent spate of murders in Munich, and I'm hoping you can help me."

Maurice shrugged. "I left Munich nearly two years ago. I haven't been near the place since then."

"I need to ask you some questions about 1931."

Maurice picked up his gloves and got to his feet. "I have nothing to say about that. The Geli case is closed. Why dredge all that up again? Why do you think we're meeting on the top of an Austrian Alp?"

"I'm not interested in the old case. I'm just looking for some background information. I can pay."

Maurice sat down again. Saxon placed 100 Reichsmark on the table. Maurice swept up the notes and tucked them inside one of his gloves.

"One of my murder victims is called Frau Henrietta Happeck. Can you confirm that she worked at Prinzregentenplatz 16 in September 1931?"

"She was the housekeeper at the time, yes."

"Who else was present when Geli died?"

"The boss and I were in Nuremburg. Hoffmann, the photographer was with us, so I can't be sure who was there, but Geli had a close companion, a young woman who tutored her from the age of about 15, when the boss took her – under his wing. She may have been in the apartment when Geli died. Her name was Maxine."

"Maxine Weiss?"

"That's right."

Saxon's heart did a somersault. "Was there anybody else present at the time? What about Maria Kazinski?"

"Never heard of her."

"Did the Führer ever use the services of a prostitute?"

"Not that I know of, but you should ask Georg Bell about that." He got to his feet and put his gloves. "I have to go."

"Where can I find this Georg Bell?"

"Speak to Michael Gerlich." And Maurice swept out the door. Saxon watched him clip on his skis and head off down the mountain.

The return journey down in the cable cars was a blur of happy skiers and stunning vertiginous views. Saxon now had a positive link between victims 2 and 3 and a possible motive for their deaths. He knew Michael Gerlich, editor of the anti-Nazi newspaper *The Straight Path*, one of a handful of journalists who consistently questioned the Party's anti-Semitism and dubious tactics. If Gerlich could supply the missing link to tie Maria Kazinski to the Geli case he might be able to solve the case.

He took the train back to Munich, arriving at the apartment well after dark.

He kissed Ruth. "How's the baby?" he whispered, peering at the infant asleep in his cot.

"Little Samuel's been well, but he refuses to sleep more than four hours between feeds. I'm exhausted. I'm going to put him on a bottle."

Samuel. Good name, he thought. "Remember what the doctor said, Ruth. Breast milk is best for young babies."

"What would he know? He's never had to undergo torture like this. I've got to get a night's unbroken sleep."

#

The early morning fog was there to welcome Saxon back to the city.

"Where were you?" roared Kriminaldirektor Mydas. "I've had Kratschik in my ear for the past 24 hours demanding to talk to you."

"I took a short trip to Austria."

Mydas clenched his sausage fingers into fists. "This is no time for holidays, Saxon, what were you thinking?"

"I was following a line of enquiry, sir."

"What line of enquiry? No," he held up a podgy palm. "Don't tell me. I don't want to know. Just get in touch with the Standartenführer and get him off my back."

Saxon called Glasser into his office and filled him in on the results of his trip. Glasser ran to the archives and returned carrying a thin file with the name Georg Bell on it.

They went through the file together. After the War, Bell found work in Munich as an electrical engineer. In 1931 he was appointed personal secretary to Ernst Röhm, Chief of Staff of the Brownshirts. The latest entry in the file was dated June 1931. An unsubstantiated report from a police informant, it stated that Bell was now head of the intelligence service of that organisation.

"He's some sort of spy!" said Glasser.

Saxon grunted. "So it would seem, but there's no mention of any direct contact with the Führer. Look into it. See what more you can find out about the man, and get me his current address."

The telephone rang. Saxon picked it up without thinking.

"Where the hell have you been?" Kratschik's voice had lost its oiliness. It was sharp enough to cut through steel.

"I was chasing a lead, sir," Saxon replied.

"Tell me about that later. I have a warrant for you to search Freudl's home."

"We conducted that search already. We found nothing."

"I want you to do it again. Be more careful this time."

#

The old lady was incredulous when Saxon, Glasser and six uniformed Orpo policemen knocked on her door. Saxon showed her the warrant.

"Not again! I'm still cleaning up after your last search." She held a mop in her hand.

Glasser said, "Stand aside, mother."

"I'm not your mother." She brandished her mop like a weapon.

Saxon asked to speak with Freudl, but the headmaster was at the school.

The uniforms dispersed around the upper floors; Glasser and Saxon took the ground floor. Within minutes Glasser discovered a pane of glass missing from a French window in a back parlour.

"Someone broke in last night," said Frau Freudl.

"Did you report it to the police?"

"No. Nothing was taken."

Five minutes after that one of the uniforms called for Glasser to come to a bedroom on the third floor. Glasser bounded up the stairs. Saxon followed at a more leisurely pace.

Saxon entered the bedroom to find Glasser and the Orpo man peering into a leather trunk full of clothing dating from the previous century. Three items of clothing were modern – two shirts and a woman's undergarment – and they were covered in blood.

"These weren't here three days ago," said Glasser to Saxon.

"You're certain?"

"Yes, I'm certain. I searched this room myself."

Saxon took the three bloodied items downstairs and showed them to Frau Freudl. "Whose are these, Frau Freudl?"

"I've never seen them before. Where did you find them?"

"We found them in a trunk in the front bedroom on the left on the third floor. Whose room is that?"

"No one's. It's a big house. We don't use the upper floors."

Saxon took the bloodied clothing to the morgue. Medical Examiner Valachek passed the garments to his assistant with instructions to test the blood type on the garments to see if it matched that of any of the victims.

"It would be helpful if the tests took a couple of days," said Saxon.

"Understood," Valachek replied, handing over a copy of the second and third autopsy reports. Saxon found an empty desk and sat down to read them. They made depressing reading.

\#

Glasser said, "That clothing was planted by someone."

"Someone like Kratschik?"

Glasser chewed the inside of his cheek. "I don't like the way this is going, Boss. He's leading us by the nose, forcing us into a corner."

Saxon gave his assistant a cigarette. "Let's wait and see what Valachek comes up with. Maybe the blood on the clothing won't match any of the victims." He put his hat on and strode to the door. "In the meantime, concentrate on Georg Bell. Get me an address."

"Where are you going, Boss?"

"To talk to an old friend."

\#

The office of the newspaper, *The Straight Path*, was deserted, the door swinging crazily from one hinge, the contents of the file cabinets strewn around the floor, the drawers of all the desks smashed and emptied. Saxon picked up a few pieces of paper, but found nothing of interest. He was on nodding terms with Herr Hoffmann, a tailor whose workshop was in the next office. He asked an office boy there what had happened.

"Brownshirts," said the boy. "They came yesterday and took most of the staff away."

"Where can I find someone who worked here?"

"Fräulein Vassan lives somewhere in Betzenweg."

There were only two apartment blocks on Betzenweg, and it didn't take him long to find Fräulein Vassan. He remembered her as a bright, cheerful girl, but now she appeared pale as a ghost with wild, terrified eyes.

Her hands shook as she closed the door.

She remembered Saxon from his occasional visits to the office. Under gentle prompting from Saxon she took him through the events of the day before. The Brownshirts had stormed the office. They had beaten Herr Gerlich and two other journalists and ransacked the office. Gerlich and the others were arrested and taken away.

"Do you know where they were taken?"

She shook her head. "No."

"Did they give a reason for the arrests?"

"No, but Herr Gerlich had been worried for several weeks that something like this might happen. He was working on a big story..."

"The Geli Raubal story?"

"You know about that? The Brownshirts removed boxes and boxes of papers. I'm sure they took everything he had on the case."

She buried her head in her hands and wept. Her shoulders shook. Saxon handed her a handkerchief. She took it, wiped her face, and blew her nose. He fetched a glass of water from the kitchen.

She handed back the handkerchief. "Forgive me."

He gave her the water. "You've had a severe shock. My questions are not helping. I'll leave you."

She looked up. "What will happen to Herr Gerlich and the others?"

The Brownshirts operated outside the law, and with Hitler in power there was little prospect of anything being done to rein them in, but he said, "They should be released fairly quickly. They have committed no crime."

He put his hat on. She accompanied him to the door. "One last thing I need to ask you before I go, Fräulein: Do you know where I could contact Georg Bell? I believe Herr Gerlich spoke to him about the case."

The wide-eyed look of terror returned. "I know nothing about him, sorry, Kommissar."

She closed the door sharply, leaving Saxon with the overwhelming feeling of a job only half done, like a half-eaten meal.

Chapter 4

"Georg Bell has gone to ground," said Glasser. "If he's half the spy I think he is. We'll never find him."

"Put out the word that we want to talk to him about something that happened in 1931. If he gets a hint that we're looking at the Geli Raubal case again we won't need to find him. He'll find us."

"I don't see that, Boss."

"Trust me. He's a spy, and spies are endlessly curious. He won't be able to resist."

Kratschik called on the telephone. "I trust you have Bart Freudl in custody."

"No, sir, we have no evidence against the headmaster."

"Your search uncovered blood-stained garments belonging to the three victims, I believe. What more evidence do you need?"

"We found some blood-stained garments, that's true, sir. But we won't know if they relate to the murders until the Medical Examiner has completed his tests."

Kratschik slammed the telephone down. Saxon went home for the weekend, wondering where Kratschik was getting his information from.

#

On Monday morning Saxon found the results of the laboratory tests on his desk. As expected, the blood taken from the three garments matched the blood groups of the three victims. This evidence was not conclusive, but, given the links between Freudl and two of the victims, it couldn't be ignored.

Saxon looked at his telephone, which remained like a silent brooding hen on his desk, ready to lay an egg at any moment.

"Nothing from Kratschik this morning?" said Glasser.

"Thank the gods. Better bring Freudl in. We can't delay any longer."

Glasser left and returned with the headmaster in tow. Saxon heard the tirade of abuse as they entered the stationhouse and gave him a few moments to settle before starting the interview.

He went through Freudl's alibis again for the nights of the three murders. His mother was his only corroboration for all three nights. Saxon presented the headmaster with the new evidence of the blood-stained clothing.

"That's preposterous. You found no such evidence during your first search."

"We must have missed it."

"You can't really believe that! We had a burglary the night before your second search. You saw the broken windowpane. Nothing was taken. It's obvious that someone broke in to the house and planted that new evidence. Someone is trying to frame me for crimes that I didn't commit."

Saxon couldn't disagree with Freudl's analysis, but without solid alibis he would stand little chance in the courts of the Third Reich. Things were changing fast. Already, the police were no longer the sole guardians of the law as they were subordinate to the Schutzstaffel. And, under pressure from the Party, the courts could no longer be relied on for the impartial administration of justice.

He pressed Freudl to reveal any knowledge of Frau Happeck, the second victim. Freudl insisted that he had never met the woman. Saxon put Freudl in a holding cell and called Glasser into his office.

"Our friend is in a bind. With the evidence we have the courts will surely send him to the scaffold." Saxon shuddered. The scaffold was no more than a figure of speech, and they both knew it. Since Hitler had come to power the Munich courts had sentenced several people to death by guillotine.

"What if we keep him here until the killer strikes again, Boss? That would strengthen his hand."

"I think we need to take more direct action than that."

"Like what?"

"You do realise whoever planted those three garments must be the killer, and whoever he is, he's a worried man."

"Kratschik."

"Yes, Kratschik may be the killer or it may be his son. Find out where the Standartenführer lives, but do nothing until I give the word."

Ruth called on the telephone at midday. "Samuel's not well, *Schatzl*. I need you here." Saxon could hear the infant crying in the background.

"Take him to the doctor if he's ill. What can I do for him?"

"You're his father. I need you with me. Frau Snydacker next door has been no help at all."

"I'm not sure I can—" She cut the line.

Frau Snydacker? He racked his brain. Frau Snydacker was the neighbour who died last year! And Ruth never called him *Schatzl*. The hairs stood up on the back of his neck. Ruth was sending him a message. She was not alone. Someone had invaded their home. He called Glasser.

"I think there's somebody with my wife."

"Where is she?"

"She's in the apartment at home, but I received a strange telephone call from her." He opened his desk, pulled out his holster and strapped it on. He loaded his handgun with ammunition and put it in the holster. Glasser did the same, and they left the office together.

"I'll go in alone," said Saxon as they drew up outside his apartment building. "You wait here. If I need you I'll blow my whistle."

Ruth and baby Samuel were sleeping. He shook her awake.

"You had someone with you. What happened?"

"A stranger. A big man with a long jaw. He told me to call you on the telephone, to ask you to come home. I mentioned poor Frau Snydacker. I tried to warn you…"

"That worked well, but where is the stranger now?"

"He said he'd meet you in Marienplatz in time for the chimes at 11 o'clock. He said you should come alone."

#

Marienplatz was teeming with tourists and locals. At exactly 11 o'clock the clock rang and all eyes turned to the Rathaus clock tower as the glockenspiel display began. Saxon cast his eyes over the people around him, but failed to identify anyone even remotely sinister-looking.

Then a hand gripped his arm. "You were looking for me, Kommissar."

He spun around and found himself face to face with a smiling face with a long jaw. He was older than the picture on his file and his hairline had receded like an ocean before a tsunami, but Saxon recognised Georg Bell. "Herr Bell, I should arrest you for breaking into my home and frightening my wife."

"Forgive me," said Bell. "I didn't mean to frighten her."

"I need to ask you a few questions about 1931 in Prinzregentenplatz."

"Anything I can do to help, Kommissar."

"You are aware that both Frau Happeck and Maxine Weiss were killed in the last seven days?"

"Yes. I was greatly saddened by their deaths."

"They were the last two of three identical murders. The first was a prostitute called Maria Kazinski. She worked in a brothel..."

"What is your question?"

"Is there any connection between the Geli suicide and Maria Kazinski?"

"None that I know of, and it wasn't suicide."

"You gave information about the Geli... affair to Michael Gerlich. You must know that Gerlich has been arrested, his records removed? I assume Gerlich spoke with Frau Happeck and Maxine Weiss?"

Bell nodded. "Yes."

"So that's why they died?"

"Very probably. Gerlich was about to blow the top off the whole case."

"What can you tell me about his findings?'

"I can tell you that Geli was murdered and he had the evidence to prove it."

"Gerlich could name the murderer?"

"Why do you think the Brownshirts arrested him and killed the only two people present in the apartment?"

"Were you involved in the killing?"

"Not directly."

"You weren't in the apartment when Geli Raubal died?"

"No, but I supplied the key that allowed the SS to gain access."

"Give me a name. Give me something – anything."

"I can't. I wouldn't last a week." He looked around nervously. The chimes were nearing the end. "Goodbye, Kommissar. I wish you good fortune with your investigation. Just remember that not everything is as it appears."

And Georg Bell disappeared into the crowd.

#

Saxon returned to the office with Georg Bell's words ringing in his head. He invited his assistant into his office, closed the door, and ran through his meeting with Georg Bell.

When he'd finished, Glasser said, "He confirmed that Frau Happeck and Maxine were witnesses to the killing of Geli Raubal?"

"Perhaps not witnesses, but they were present in the apartment at the time. The only ones, he said."

"And the assassin was SS?"

"Yes. We must assume the killing was ordered by the Führer himself."

"That's dynamite, Boss. It could bring the Nazi government down."

"Undoubtedly. But without Gerlich and his records we have nothing."

"What did he mean, 'not everything is as it appears'?" said Glasser.

"I don't know, but I want to take another look at the Medical Examiner's reports." He opened the three reports and spread them out on his desk.

"What are we looking for, Boss?"

"Professor Valachek mentioned that all three victims had been struck on the head. Frau Happeck and the teacher, Maxine, had been killed by the initial blow, but Maria Kazinski was alive but unconscious until the end of the mutilations." He read Professor Valachek's breakdown of the gruesome mutilations and could find no differences.

Glasser said, "Listen to this, Boss." He read from the first report: "The blade used to kill Maria Kazinski was short and narrow, like a dagger, 15 cm long." He picked up a page from the second autopsy report: "The weapon that killed Frau Happeck was at least 30 cm long and had a broad blade, like a rapier."

Saxon leafed through the third report and found the description of the weapon used. "This one was long and broad. The last two were identical, the first was a different weapon!"

In his excitement, Saxon patted his jacket pockets looking for a cigarette. Glasser opened a packet and they lit up together in a cloud of smoke.

"We're looking for two killers," said Glasser. "The second and third murders were political, the first killing was something else."

"You're right," said Saxon, "but still, the three killings are connected. The last two were copies of the first. The SS intended us to lay the blame for all three murders on the killer of Maria Kazinski."

"And the three blood-stained garments pointed the fingers squarely at the headmaster," said Glasser. "I wonder why they chose him?"

"I identified him as a possible suspect, remember. The SS probably want to remove him from his post and put one of their own in there. But the discovery of those garments also proves that, whoever the two killers are, they are closely connected."

"Like father and son?" said Glasser.

Saxon stubbed out his cigarette. "If we bring Kratschik junior in for questioning, the consequences don't bear thinking about."

Glasser said, "We could do nothing, Boss."

"And let a brutal murderer go free? I don't think so. And anyway, Kratschik is insisting that we solve the case. If we fail we'll be back in uniform by morning, arresting carthorses for fouling the streets."

"What if we charge Freudl?"

"He would face the guillotine. An innocent man. Could you live with that?"

"No."

"This is Zugzwang," said Saxon, gloomily.

"Zugzwang, Boss?"

"It's a chess term. It means we are obliged to move, but whatever move we make will lose us the game.

#

Saxon shivered as he entered SS headquarters clutching a briefcase. Entry to the building was through a courtyard at the rear of Schellingstrasse 50. Up until 1931 this had been the Nazi Party's national headquarters, and all the signs were there – the eagle over the lintel, the shrine in the vestibule where the bloodflag used to hang, and swastikas everywhere you looked.

He was made to wait the customary 20 minutes before being shown into the office of SS-Standartenführer Karl Kratschik.

"Take a seat, Kommissar." It was an order, not an invitation.

The office was spacious enough to accommodate a small table and four chairs. Saxon took one of those.

Kratschik joined him at the table. "Why has Bart Freudl not been charged?" said the SS man as he settled his behind into a chair.

"I believe Herr Freudl is innocent, Herr Standartenführer. We now have compelling evidence against another man." Saxon opened his briefcase, took out the school photograph and placed it on the table in front of the SS man. "This individual, here. He calls himself 'Heinrich.'"

Kratschik took one look at the face in the picture and blanched.

Saxon continued, "We have yet to identify the young man, but anyone present at the school when this photograph was taken should be able to name him."

Kratschik picked up the photograph and took it to his desk. "Join me here." An invitation, not an order this time. Saxon took the chair facing the desk.

Kratschik opened a silver cigarette box and offered it to Saxon. "What evidence do you have against this man?"

Saxon took a cigarette, but the lighter was out of reach on Kratschik's desk.

"He was Maria Kazinski's last customer on the night she was killed, and he has a reputation for violence. It shouldn't be difficult to break him down once we have him under lock and key."

"You can connect him to the other two victims?"

"The teacher, Frau Limburg, is there in the photograph."

"Ah, but can you link him to the third victim?"

"As I said, Herr Standartenführer, once we have him under interrogation..."

"What of the blood-stained clothing you found? That clearly linked the schoolmaster to the three killings."

"That evidence was false. The killer broke in to Herr Freudl's home and placed it there."

Kratschik sat forward in his chair and put his hands together, his fingertips to his lips.

"You are married, Kommissar?"

"Yes, sir."

"Children?"

"Just one child, a boy, three weeks old."

"I have one son. He leaves today to join the Reichswehr, his grandfather's regiment, based in the north."

"Congratulations, sir."

Kratschik stood. He slid the school photograph into a desk drawer. "You have done a remarkable job, Saxon, and I thank you. But you need do nothing more. Send me the entire file. The Schutzstaffel will take over the investigation from here."

Saxon placed his unlit cigarette in his breast pocket. He closed the clasp on his briefcase and got to his feet. "I have never abandoned an investigation before completing it, Herr Standartenführer."

"You wife's name is Ruth?"

An icy finger touched the back of Saxon's neck.

"Yes, sir."

"Isn't that a Jewish name?"

THE END

ABOUT THE AUTHOR

JJ Toner is a full time writer. He lives in Ireland. Look for his Black Orchestra series of WW2 spy stories. Find him at https://www.jjtoner.com/